THE COWBOY
— AND —
THE WITCH

The Witch Queen of New Orleans

AMY EXSTERSTEIN

Copyright © 2025 Amy Exsterstein.

All rights reserved. No part of this book may be reproduced, stored, or transmitted by any means—whether auditory, graphic, mechanical, or electronic—without written permission of both publisher and author, except in the case of brief excerpts used in critical articles and reviews. Unauthorized reproduction of any part of this work is illegal and is punishable by law.

ISBN: 979-8-89419-677-0 (sc)
ISBN: 979-8-89419-678-7 (hc)
ISBN: 979-8-89419-679-4 (e)

Because of the dynamic nature of the Internet, any web addresses or links contained in this book may have changed since publication and may no longer be valid. The views expressed in this work are solely those of the author and do not necessarily reflect the views of the publisher, and the publisher hereby disclaims any responsibility for them.

One Galleria Blvd., Suite 1900, Metairie, LA 70001
(504) 702-6708

SUMMARY

Terra was destined to become the next witch queen of New Orleans Louisiana. Except Mayor Andrew McShane wants her whole linage gone so he can control the human realm as well as the magical one. Traveling back in time was her only chance of survival, and that's when destiny stepped in. Terra's world collided with the rugged sexy cowboy, Boone and made an alliance that she hoped would save them all before it was too late.

CONTENTS

Prologue vii

Chapter 1	"Forbidden Spell of Travel"	1
Chapter 2	"Doom, Gloom, and Boone"	4
Chapter 3	"Home Sweet Home?"	7
Chapter 4	"No Rest for the Witches"	9
Chapter 5	"A Time for Change is Coming"	11
Chapter 6	"West We Geaux"	16
Chapter 7	"No Hide, Only Seek"	19
Chapter 8	"No Place Like Home"	22
Chapter 9	"Blood of the Innocent"	26
Chapter 10	"My Side of the Pond"	29
Chapter 11	"The Calvary has Arrived"	34
Chapter 12	"Finders Keepers"	36
Chapter 13	"Beware of the Swamp Witch"	41
Chapter 14	"The Awakening"	45
Chapter 15	"Come Out, Come Out Wherever You Are"	49
Chapter 16	"Home Sweet Home"	52
Chapter 17	"The Count Down"	55
Chapter 18	"All Isn't Fair in Love or War"	61
Chapter 19	"Purple is for Bravery"	67

Epilogue 69

PROLOGUE

October 3, 1877

The smell of smoke and burning flesh filled the night air. The prisoners all screamed their innocence as they were lit on fire one by one for their crimes of witchcraft and trying to assassinate the Mayor of New Orleans. Their screams travelled for miles over the bayou waters.

Dressed in long black hooded cloaks with silver crosses around their necks, the hench man began reading them their last rites. "The Great state of Louisiana finds you guilty and hear by sentences you to death for your crimes against its people!"

Mayola's long beautiful black hair blowing in the breeze and her once long red gown was now tattered and torn. With her hands tied up over her head to a post she squeezes her eyes shut trying to block out the pain.

"He says to tell you he will miss you tremendously." The henchmen smiled. Opening her eyes to see his commander sneering back at her. There was only one thing left she could do. Pulling together what was left of her strength, Mayola stared at the henchmen and townspeople.

"I Mayola Everleigh Poyadeaux, gift my powers and my book of shadows to my only child, Terra Marie Poyadeaux !" Mayola screams into the night for all to hear as the flames engulf her battered body.

A flash of light left her body to travel through the magical realm to Terra. So mote it be. The towns people cheered and snickered as her screams died down.

Looking up at the henchman one last time. "One day you will pay for this, for one day my child shall rule, and you will obey her." Mayola whispers into the wind as she slowly turns to ashes.

CHAPTER 1

"FORBIDDEN SPELL OF TRAVEL"

October 3, 1877

"If I leave now, they won't be able to catch me." Terra whispered, tears overflowing as she fumbles through the drawers of her mother's house looking for her book of shadows. "I need that spell! Ancestors, please help me!" she begs. A soft glow appears under the cabinet. The feeling of her mother nearby and a sharp pain in her right hand, she knew what her mother had done. Terra opens the door and starts pulling up the boards. With sad crying eyes and a deep pain in her chest she knows she must be strong if she's going to save them. Finding the book and quickly flipping through the pages." Here it is! "The Forbidden spell of travel. "Mother! They will pay for this!" She promised out loud. Terra begins to read holding her belly knowing the life growing there is salvation for everyone. Closing her eyes, and clearing her mind, Terra lifted her arms in the air, palms to the sky, Terra begins chanting....

"Hear these words,
Hear the rhyme,
heed the hope within my mind's eye,
Send me back to where I will find,
what I wish in this place and time."

Blue flames started erupting around her. Her mind's eye could see a clock going backwards faster and faster as the ground started shaking. Terra closed her eyes and repeated the incantation until she heard voices telling her to run.

"Terra! Terra! Open your eyes child! Run! Run and never look back!" Terra jumped up ith her bag held closely to her swollen belly and took off south of the cottage. Letting her intuition guide her and following the soft humming of a song but not understanding the words. Terra finally made it to a clearing in the woods where a soft light illuminated a small round door. The door overflowed with its colorful beauty and scents of Aster, Golden rods, coneflower, hydrangeas, sunflowers, and dahlia. She looks behind the door, but it doesn't seem to go anywhere. And yet the door seemed to be alive, breathing and silently waiting.

"I've never seen anything like this". Then she hears giggling and chanting that sounded like a small child.

"Mi la fe"
We are fae,
"Bi le te"
Here our words,
"Ye ti un pa"
Follow the sound of our voice.....
"Ye ty ye"
Come this way,
"Bre ty ye"
Survive this day.

The low humming, the feeling of calming, and warmth engulfed Terra. The doorway of flowers seems to call to her and there are small things flying all around her. Terra felt lighter and more comfortable as she walked towards the door. It was now dusk. Behind her she could hear the townspeople coming for her. And there was nowhere to hide. She must trust her heart, or everything would be lost. Trusting her magic and her ancestors, Terra took a deep breath, held her swollen belly and leaped through the door. The chanting of the spell continued as she was sucked through the time warp. Racing lights and faces went by as she was thrown towards her destiny. It seemed to go on forever.

"Terra....Terra..." she could hear her mother calling to her.

"Mom! Mom! Where are you? "Terra pleaded. In her mind's eye she could see her beautiful mother, so young, playing with a small child laughing and running by a river. It felt safe here. She could feel the sun on her face and the love in her heart for her mother all around her.

Right beyond the tree line behind them she could see yellow glowing eyes watching them. As Terra got closer, she could see those eyes were attached to a huge white wolf!

The wolf seems to be intrigued or just watching, not really threatening. Terra starts to feel a pull towards the wolf. The wolf stares right at Terra then turns around to trot off. He turns back around to make sure she is following. The air starts to turn musty, and she finds herself running behind the huge wolf! After a few minutes Terra stops and listens. She could hear the blood rushing through her ears. Losing sight of which way the wolf went, she hit her knees and vomited. Spinning and running and the sudden stop was overwhelming. Exhaustion is starting to take over.

"I just need to lay down for a moment". Sitting at the base of a huge oak tree pulling her shawl around her." Just rest my eyes for a moment..."

CHAPTER 2

"DOOM, GLOOM, AND BOONE"

October 4, 1803

Looking at the sun it's about 6 am. Exhausted after being out all night delivering the 8 baby calves, Boone heads back towards the barn to feed up. Time to eat and take a nap.

"Boone! Boone!" Hank was calling as he came over the hill. Boone turns his horse around to ride back towards the river.

"What is it, Hank?" Boone asked as his eyes widened as he got closer.

"Seems to be a woman" Boone says through clenched teeth.

"Well, we might as well bring her inside, it's going to rain soon." Hank insisted.

"What? She's not our responsibility!" Boone whispered angrily.

"Is she breathing son? "Hank looked at him with one eyebrow raised sarcastically.

"I believe so." Boone seemed tired and even more annoyed. But he knew Hank was right, and he was raised better than that. But the last thing Boone needed right now was a stranger upsetting the quite life he had built on this patch of dirt for the last 3 years.

"Ma'am, ma'am." Boone gently shakes Terra. She opens her eyes mumbling about a book or something. He was mesmerized by her beautiful tan face, and long dark wavy hair. Although her clothing was odd, she did look like a local. Turning his eyes back upwards, Warm honey brown eyes were staring back at him that reminded him of a good bottle of whiskey. Man, he sure could use a glass of that right now.

Coming from a long line of strong Cajun women with a linage of voodoo and a raw magical life, nothing could have prepared Terra for the emotions she felt when she opened her eyes and was staring into the most beautiful pair of crystal-clear blue eyes she had ever seen. Realizing she was struggling to stand, Boone reached down to help her up and to his horror he realized she was carrying a child. Boone and Hank helped Terra on the horse. Boone climbed on the horse behind her. It had been a long time since Boone held a woman or even been this close to one. Holding her to his chest he slowly walked the horse all the way back home.

June 1, 1799

"Push, Tilly!" The midwife urged. "We have to get this baby out now!"

"I can't go anymore." Crying and sweaty. Her beautiful blonde hair was now matted up to the side of her neck. Tilly was starting to bleed. "Please can we stop? "She cried. "It's been hours. I don't feel her moving anymore." Completely exhausted and out of breath. Tilly's face was slowly draining in color. "Get my husband."

The midwife ran to the kitchen. "Boone come with me please. She is asking for you." Running to the back room. Boone could see how pale she was from the door.

"Tilly!" Boone kneels next to her wiping her face with a towel. "Hi honey. Tell me how to fix this. Tell me what I need to do. Please." Boone begged her. Tears overflowing onto his tan face.

"My love, my Boone." Tilly put her tiny hand in his. "I will always be with you. I promise we will come visit you in your dreams." She smiled weakly.

"How can I save you? Please don't leave me." Boone held her hand to his forehead bowing in prayer like he saw the villagers doing on Sunday mornings.

"Someone help us!" Boone cried. "Please help! Tilly! Don't leave me. Tilly wake up! Wake up! I need you!" Laying his head on her chest he could no longer tell if there was any life left there. Boone threw his head back and let out a sound so loud it shook the ground.

The midwife came running in the room. Whatever she saw in Boone's eyes had her backing out of the room and going back down the hallway. She took off running once she cleared the front door.

Waking up shaking his head. Boone was now awake and miserable as ever thinking of the pregnant woman sleeping on the other side of his house. Boone decided to get up to make dinner. He needed something to occupy his mind after that nightmare.

CHAPTER 3

"Home sweet Home?"

October 4, 1803

Terra wakes up to the delicious aromas of something sweet and her stomach starts to rumble. Looking around the room and out the window .... seems familiar, sort of. It's cool and humid here. Even though it's dark outside it seems a little too dark inside. Hearing the faint sounds of men talking, Terra walks towards them not sure what to expect but knowing she needs food and a bathroom.

"Well look who's awake. I'm Hank."

"Hi, I'm Terra. Can you point me towards the bathroom please?"

"Sure, right this way. "Hank smiles as he leads her outside to another building with a makeshift toilet and a huge tub in the center of the room. "Take all the time you need; dinner is ready when you're done." Hank smiled warmly. Terra thanked him as she closed the door and slid the wood plank in place.

The room was nice and cozy with a fire going, and the water was perfect. The relief of sitting here caused the tears to start falling. "I may not know where we are or what's in store, but we are safe for now little one. "Something is different. Is it the air? No, it still smells like home. Is it the out-of-date log cabin? Are those real Cowboys? Oh well, I can't quit put my finger on it, I'm so tired."

Boone is impatiently waiting for her to come back inside to eat. It's been at least 30 minutes. "I need sleep and a splash off myself. This is why I'm still single." Boone says to himself with a dramatic eyeroll.

"Ok" Terra thought holding up the garb he left for her. 'How do i even put this on? Is this a dress? An apron? "Oh, never mind as she eyes something much better hanging on the chair.

Boone's laughter could be heard two parishes over as his eyes quickly swept the 5 foot nothing in his dad's trousers walking through the back door. Her wet hare hanging down to her waist with black pants and a beige button up shirt barley masking the protruding nipples that threatened to be exposed. "What are you wearing?" Boone asked trying to hide the gleam in his eyes. But Terra noticed.

" I'm starved." she said ignoring his fun. "And besides it's the only thing that fits at the moment. "Terra looked down at her clothes thinking they looked fine.

With a shrug, she sat down and started to eat. Oh my!" she moaned." This is the most delicious pie I have ever had." As she ate her fill, Boone stared at her in wonder.

"Where did you come from? "He asked suddenly. Terra stiffened and sat up knowing this was coming and he had all the right to ask.

"Can we talk tomorrow? I've been through a lot lately...." She sounded so sad. "What day is it? "She asked. Boone looked confused but brushed it off as pregnancy stuff.

"October 4th ma'am." Terra smiled at how polite he is.

"Thank you for taking care of me. I promise not to stay long. I just need some rest. "She smiled with heavy eyelids fighting to stay open. As she lay in bed holding her book of shadows and thinking of her next move, she drifted off to sleep and dreamed of what she hoped would save them.

CHAPTER 4

"NO REST FOR THE WITCHES"

Now I lay me down to sleep,
the wolves and witches start to we
Open their eyes to show me the way,
They ask for a sacrifice on Samhain.

Terra sat straight up in bed, sweat beading down her back. 3am, the witching hour. She knew it was telling her the answer she sought. Walking to the window to lookout, she sees something written on the pane.

To save them you must seek,
The brown one by the river where he weeps.
The bottle in the trunk is the message you must receive,
The day of Samhain is not your friend,
When the veil is lowered,
The next day is his kin.

"Oh great!" A riddle of craziness is exactly what I don't need. Terra cries in frustration. Ok I have about 3 weeks to figure this out before this child is born that was bestowed upon me and save the future of not 1 but all the worlds! Got it! Easy Peasy! This is fine, everything will be fine. Tears fell down her cheeks until sleep found her once again.

"Mommyyy.... Mommyyyy. I'm here mommy. Mommy open your eyes. It's ok. I love you."

Terra wakes. It's so quiet. It's almost daylight now. "Hello, is someone there?" Something is off. Looking around Terra sees a slight movement by the closet that has her on full alert now. Did something move? Smells like mint and lilac in here." Hello?" Terra whispered. Not sure if she imagined it or if...

"Hi! I'm Macki! "A tiny, winged fairy with a purple mohawk that is way too eager to speak. She waves and smiles brightly with her pointy ears and even pointer fanged teeth..

A little unsure of what to do, Terra smiles back. "Hi, I'm Ter...."

"Terra, yes, I know all about you. I have been assigned to you, and I'm here to help guide you on your journey." Macki stands tall, back straight and salutes.

"Hi, Macki. Can we start with where we are?"

"Well, you kind of ended up in the past about 75 years or so. But don't worry, we are still in Louisiana. And I have your amulet, next we get the map, oh and then the eclipse of course, and then the veil needs to drop....

Terra eyes are wide open now.

"But don't worry, Macki is here to guide you." She stood as tall and proud as she could just like in fairy camp.

"Whoa, whoa, whoa slow down." Terra says waving her hands. "First, we need a plan. Then I need to figure how to do this with just the 2 of us, not to mention I will be having a witch of my own soon." Terra is now panting as the realization is setting in that she is back in time with a fairy, 2 cowboys, and very soon a baby.

CHAPTER 5

"A TIME FOR CHANGE IS COMING"

October 5, 1877

"Where is she? I want her found! Now!" Scream the Mayor of New Orleans.

"Well Mr. McShane sir, I mean Andrew sir, ummmm Mr. Mayor sir.... Says the tiny troll, I Think Miss Terra has disappeared... but.... but ...but I have ears and eyes looking for her everywhere sir, please don't kill me. Hugo says shaking as McShane glares down at the 2foot troll, with glassy deranged eyes.

"You have 5 days to find her, or you will be the one missing. He whispers so low it sent more shivers down Hugo's tiny body.

"Yes sir." Hugo slumped his shoulders and ran away.

October 6,1803

Boone awoke to whispering or singing or maybe it's the wind.

" Bre te Ty de"
Survive this day...

"I guess it's time to get started." Boone grumbles as he starts making breakfast and getting ready for the day. Something caught his attention in the hallway. Getting up to inspect the darkness there, he heard a cough come from Terra's room. Walking closer to her door, he heard her get out of bed and start walking towards him. He put his hand up to knock as she pulled the door open. Terra yelped just loud enough to have Hank coming out of his room across the hallway.

"Breakfast is ready." Boone mumbles walking back to the kitchen.

Hank smiled brightly at Terra and her ever growing belly. After breakfast Terra asked Boone, "So do you have any huge trees on the property near a river?"

Boone stared at her suspiciously not sure what to think of a woman in men's britches snooping around his property. "May I ask why? "Boone raised an eyebrow.

"Seems I might have lost something on my journey, and I think I remember a large tree I needed to stop and rest by." She offered not sure if he believed her.

"No disrespect ma'am, but i don't believe a woman in your condition should be running along the countryside alone. It's dangerous out there. "Boone said a matter a fact.

Knowing she couldn't disagree. Terra smiled really big." Well, I would love the company if you aren't too busy today. Please? "She asked as sweetly as she could. Blinking her pretty brown eyes.

Knowing he was defeated, he agreed. Mainly out of curiosity. It had nothing to do with how beautiful she is or her smile or how intoxicating she smelled. Mint, or lavender? Both?

With her fae amulet around her neck and her book of shadows in her bag along with a few herbs to aid in finding something lost they set out shortly after daylight to find the tree by the river.

After 15 minutes of riding, Boone let his curiosity get the best of him. "So, are you ready to tell me what's going on?"

"I am but I don't think you're ready to hear it." After much thought Terra decided he needed the truth, because for some reason she believed he could help.

"Oh yeah?" Boone stops his horse and turns to face her. "Care to explain? "He asked, tired of the word games.

"Do you believe in things your eyes can't see? Have you ever had anything happen and it felt like a miracle or that something bigger was at work?" she asked, staring at him in wonder.

Boone took a deep breath careful with his words." I know some things can't be explained. I watched my wife and child die in childbirth and then a year later my mother died of fever. And I can't explain why I am still mad 3 years later. And I can't guess why the universe would take them away from me or why it happened so cruelly! "Boone yelled angrily. I also can't imagine why the same universe would make us cross paths. His voice lowered at that thought. He looked so far away.

Terra blinked back tears for the pain he had been through that she understood all too well. Yes, I must be honest with him. The man he is, won't except anything less. "Very well." Terra got off her horse and walked over to Boone. Boone got off his horse and Terra took both of his hands in hers and looked him in his eyes. Boone could see her eyes starting to cloud as she started to chant.

"Mirror, mirror show me spirit unseen.
Inscribe my mind what the images mean.
Answer the question why, where, and how.
Appear to me the answer I seek, I am listening now.
So mote it be."

The sky started to rumble in the distance as Terra's eyes turned completely white, then darkened, then cleared again. Boone could feel her truth. The baby is a boy. Terra is a virgin. None of this makes any sense. Lightning strikes something in the distance, but Boone stays right where he is. Watching the townspeople chase her, her tear-streaked face running through a forest, there are small, blurred creatures running alongside her. A New scene erupts, a lady in red, a noose around her beautiful neck, fire, smoke. Then a cry rang out in the distance. Terra blinked and bloody tear ran down her cheek.

"Get on your horse now! We have to go." Boone was not sure if she said that out loud or in his mind. They went south when they heard the screams coming from the east. Both of them knowing whatever it is, it's coming for her. After what seemed like an eternity they came to a river. "We have about a 30-minute head start before they catch us. "Terra said looking back.

"What the hell was that? And what's after us?" Boone glared.

"Do you still want the truth? Terra asked.

"Yes, there is no going back after what I just saw in your eyes."

"It's the Mayor's henchmen after me. They want my whole linage to die. There has not been a male child in 4 generations until now." Terra said covering her belly.

"But why, I still don't understand." Boone is now frustrated with more questions than answers.

"Follow me." Terra points in a direction southwest of the river. It pulls to her. As the river starts to bend, she could smell something familiar." Mom!"

"Wow." says Boone. "That's the biggest willow I've ever seen."

"A Willow?" Terra asked.

"It's called a weeping Williow. The tree actually sheds small water droplets that fall like tears." Boone smiled at the tall, beautiful tree with huge lavender falls of branches and a huge dark trunk.

"Humm mm. The riddle." Terra pulls out her book.

"To save them you must seek,
the brown one by the river where he weeps.
The bottle in the trunk is the real message you must seek..."

"This is it! We found it, mom! "Terra said as she slid off her horse.
"What are we doing here? "Boone asked.
"I think I'm supposed to knock on this tree." She whispers. Terra studies the tree by running her hands over the bark and pushing on it to check for soft spots, or a door or anything that might be an entrance.

Boone follows her even though he thinks she's completely insane.

CHAPTER 6

"WEST WE GEAUX"

"**H**ugo!" An angry faced Mayor stared. "You better have good news!"

"Yes sir, Mayor sir. We found a flow of magic in the clearing at the old Metry farm road." Hugo offered.

"Excellent! Have the men fed and ready! We leave at dusk." McShane knew the window would stay open as long as the balance is off. But he needs an offering for the ones guarding it. And he knew there would be guards. "I will have an offering for them too. "He smiled deep and sure of himself.

Carefully examining the tree, Terra wasn't sure how to find the entrance. Terra knocked on the tree. Nothing. Boone tried pushing and pulling the branches. "Macki, Macki, are you here? "Terra whispered holding the amulet and rubbing the beautiful amethyst in the center.

"Who is, Macki?" Boone asked.

"She is a guide of sorts." Not sure if he could even see, Macki. A slight flutter came from above. They both looked up at dust that went right in their eyes. Sneezing and a little dizzy, the silver dust started to subside.

"Hi, Boone! I'm Macki! She sang out. Today her mohawk was purple and silver to match her eyes. Boone just stared at her in disbelief.

"Macki, how do we get in? "Terra shrugged.
Macki smiled brightly "Oh right, let's hold hands and say....

"Wo lo wi,
Wake up Willow
My ti ro"
Time to work

They chanted over and over. "Did you bring payment?" Macki asked.
"Payment for what?" Boone asked.
"For magic silly. "She smiled sweetly. Macki waits patiently as Willow grumbles awake.
"Who is here?" Willow asked.
"It's me, Willow. Terra Poyadeaux. I need your help. I believe you have a bottle of information I need. Please Willow! The fate of our worlds depends on it." Terra pleads. "What is your price?"
The Willow looks around and smiles. "I will take that horse, yes, that's what I would like." Sounding pleased with himself. The horse seemed to understand because he started walking towards the tree as if he excepted him.
Boone moaned. "That's my favorite horse! "As soon as the horse reached them the ground opened up to a staircase below. Walking down the stairs together into a dim lit cave of wonder. There were piles of gold, jewels, scrolls, and every kind of treasure you could imagine, and it went on forever.
"Only touch the treasure you seek, anything else will cause a leak. "A voice whispered.
"Did I imagine that, or was it said out loud? "Boone asked nervously. No one said a word. Barley breathing, looking around. "So, what are we looking for exactly? "Boone asked quietly.
"A glass bottle with papers in it, probably with this printed on it." Terra held up her book of shadows with the wolf's head on it.

"Ok." No denying what I can see and touch. But Boone is sweating and its so hot inside. A little dizzy too. Boone closed his eyes to catch his breath, and everything went dark. He woke to see those eyes staring down at him.

"What happened? "Terra asked with concern, filling her face.

"I don't know, but I feel strange in a good way. "He smiled back at her almost drunk on the air in here. Terra helped Boone up and looked around for a moment before he stopped and closed his eyes to inhale deeply and looked right at the bottle they needed. "There." Boone pointed. Upon careful inspection Terra knew it was the bottle she had been looking for.

"We got it! Now how do we open it? "She asked. Instinctively Boone grabs the bottle and bites his finger. A drop of blood sprang forward. Boone wiped the blood on the wolf emblem, and it started glowing. Boone and Terra looked at each other in shock. The bottle crumpled in Boone's hands.

"It's a map! "They both said together.

The Willow starts to grumble and Macki screams. "Run! We must get out before they reach the tree!"

"That way!" Boone points as they run down a huge hallway leading down another flight of stairs into a room full of murals.

Paintings on the ceilings of war with Witches and goblins, and fae, wolves, and demonlike creatures with writings they couldn't understand. The paintings of the ancient one's eyes seem to follow them. Down another hallway and up a staircase the room seemed to tunnel under a street to a wooden door. Slowly Boone pushed the door open. It was so quiet. Climbing out onto the riverbank with a small bridge next to it. Macki slammed the door shut behind her and sealed it with her beautiful singing.

"Ne mai wi sa ta der ti to du les"
No one will see this door until the dust settles

CHAPTER 7

"NO HIDE, ONLY SEEK"

"They are here somewhere." Mayor McShane stared out across the land and the river. "I can feel it."

Hugo runs to the horse by the river to smell it, but the horse runs from him in fear. Then something shiny catches his eye. He picks it up. It's a coin with a wolf head on it. "Maybe I should hold on to this." Hugo thinks his suspicions may be correct. Could it be his queen's descendant? Could this be what the world has been waiting for?

McShane walks up to the Willow to inspect the footprints that seem to disappear right into the tree itself. A smile as evil as hell itself spreads across his face. "They found it." They have the map! And we have an old friend to visit. We ride Northwest towards the lake!"

"We must get back to the ranch. We need a plan. And I want the whole story this time, Terra." Boone's voice is low and serious.

"I think you deserve that much." Terra replies completely exhausted.

"We have at least half a day ride back across the river to the lakeside. Let's stop and eat. Boone offered.

"Yes, please! "Macki smiles with her bright eyes looking back and forth hungrily. Macki zips away to hunt for food. 10 minutes later she is back with the biggest bullfrog Boone has ever seen. Sinking her little sharp fangs into the bullfrog and draining it dry. She drops the frog at Boone's feet. "Yummy!" Macki says satisfied." Yall can have the rest."

Boone picks up the frog and decides it's better than nothing. With a fire started and the frog legs grilling, Terra sat there trying to stay awake while her stomach growled. "I'm so tired." She yawns.

"We have time to rest, I don't think anyone is following us." Boone said sympathetically. Macki curls up on Terra's belly to relax.

Jumping up, Boone hears horse hooves coming.

"It's your horse, Terra! She found us!" Macki squeals with delight. The horse went right up to Boone to nudge him. He is still sad about giving up his best stud. But being able to pet his beautiful mare was a big relief.

"Oh, I can't wait to bathe and get real food!" Cried Terra.

"Not much farther, we live over that next bridge." Boone sighs with relief.

"Boone, we only have 1 week to find the contents of this map." Terra frowns. "I'm not even sure what it is, but I do know it will fix all of this."

"What is this exactly? And how am I tied to this? Boone made a circle with his arms for dramatization. There is a lot I'm missing, and a lot you're not telling me.

Macki smiled nervously and looked at Terra." Go ahead and tell him.

"Terra stared at Macki for a moment, then turned to Boone. "Ok, here goes."

"Boone. I am a witch. A creole Voodoo Witch. My mother is the descendant of one of the most powerful Voodoo queens in Louisiana. Her legacy is tied to some of the wealthiest families here. But to save our future realm we must rid it of the McShane family. My family has worked for their family for over a hundred years. I alone, now hold all their family secrets. Only their family secrets are monstrous, and they must be stopped. They have been breeding an army of monsters. My family stole some of the things they needed to finish this army. He murdered everyone involved except me. I barely got away. I woke up pregnant in his lab, so I ran!" It was a long pause before Terra said anything else. You could tell by the look on Boone's face he was weighing the things she was saying. The shock in his eyes was obvious. Then the sadness, and disbelief was there too. "They burned my mother!" Terra screamed as tears slid down her face.

Boone looked away so Terra couldn't see the concern on his face. Terra touched the back of his arm.

"I know this child will save us all, and I need your help, please!" Terra paused hoping it was enough to convince him." We must find what's on this map before they do. My family were the keepers of these monsters. It is time to stop this!" Tears were now flowing down her cheeks, pleading with him to agree to this fate. "I just know you are supposed to be here in this moment with me, I know it in my bones."

Boone stared at Terra for a long moment and ran his hands through his hair and let out a hard breath. "After everything that has happened this week, I can't deny what I have seen with my own 2 eyes. Or the way I feel. Or the way my blood turned that bottle into a map, so here's what we are going to do." Bonne said calmly." First, we must get back to my house and get supplies. And I need to talk to my father. Then we can go find this treasure...."

CHAPTER 8

"No Place Like Home"

"Tell us where they are old man, or I will gut you and leave you here strung up for them to find." McShane said in his raspy matter a fact way.

Hank is about to show him what justice is as a growl slowly left his bleeding lips. 257 isn't that old, as his eyes began to turn gold and back to bright blue. McShane stared in amusement when he realized he didn't have any silver bullets, but no matter. "This chain of silver shall keep you still for a bit while I find my treasure." Hank started screaming as the chains began burning into his skin. "Set the stable on fire." McShane instructed his commander while looking Hank in the eye.

"I will get you for this. It ain't over." Hank promised.

Boone and Terra were almost over the bridge when Boone's high sense of smell caught a whiff of smoke. Riding hard towards the barn Boone was yelling for Hank. "Dad! Dad!" Terra decided to hide under the bridge for Boone to return.

"Oh, where is it? Macki! I need you!' Terra said in a panic looking for her amulet.

"I found her!" Hugo yells through small yellow teeth. Three large men dressed in soldier gear pull Terra from under the bridge. She didn't struggle for fear of hurting the child.

"Don't do this. You don't understand what has happened. He doesn't care about you. He is trying to destroy our worlds!" Terra tried to reason with them. But Hugo nodded for them to take her.

Hugo picked up all of Terra's belongings and noticed she had a book of shadows, but when he flipped through it, he noticed the pages were blank. All of them.... But we got the girl, and the mayor will finally be pleased.

McShane met Boone at the front door. "Welcome home nephew." He smiled with utter delight.

"Where's my father?" Boone demanded.

"Oh, he's here alright, just waiting for his special son to return." Without warning, McShane shoved a 4-inch hunting knife in Boone's chest. McShane laughed as Boone crumbled to the floor.

October 10, 1877

Terra wakes up very groggy and dying of thirst. "Water." Terra said weakly. "Water. Please. "She begged.

"Hold on child. "The nurse maid came forward to help her."

"Where am I?" Terra asked.

"We at the mayor's mansion, and I am Madam Dauphine! You must be starving. Let me get you some food." She smiled kindly.

As soon as Madam walked out, Terra tried to stand, dizziness and nausea hit her. Her stomach was so empty there wasn't anything to come up. Terra lay back down worried about Boone and Macki. Did they make it? How long have I been asleep? How do I get out of here?

After dinner Terra decided to save her strength. She was going to need it.

There was a knock at the door. In came the mayor without an invitation. Walking right up to Terra.

"Good evening, Terra. "McShane said standing so close to her it sent a chill down her spine. "How are you and my son doing this evening?" His smile broadened.

Terra froze in disbelief. "Your what?" Terra asked slowly.

"That's MY seed you carry." He assured Terra.

Handsome in his own right with his blonde curls, tan skin and beautiful white teeth. Not to mention his deep blue eyes that seem familiar. Except for the red dot in them that seem to be almost moving. Maybe. Weird.

"Ever wonder how you woke up like this?" He asked. One perfectly manicured eyebrow arched in question.

"What are you saying you lunatic?" Terra demanded.

"Ha! Lunatic, maybe. Lovers? You are not my type Terra. But unfortunately for me you're the last of your linage, and a witch. And a virgin. The perfect mixture to bear the next divine. And I will be his father. "McShane said arrogantly. "My blood mixed with pure witch blood. I will be unstoppable, and this world will bow to me. "He smiled so lovingly at himself in the mirror.

"What are you besides crazy!" Terra screamed in anger.

"Oh Cher, what indeed." He bared his teeth hissing at her. McShane walked to the window and looked far away as his memories started to invade him. His eyes seemed to have a slight glow when he began to speak.

"The child of rape from a mad wolf and born to a nun of the religious cult called, Christians. She hung herself over my birthed body in the full moonlight of the winter solstice. Turning to stare at Terra, his eyes went wild. "He roared with anger and disgust.

"Because she could not bear the sight of my hairy body and pointy ears!" He yelled, ripping his shirt open to reveal the scars that covered his battered torso. Some scars were so deep she was sure the organs must be missing. Terra backed up in fear. "I've used my blood to make many children as of late. My beautiful half breeds. McShane grabbed Terra's hand and images started flashing through her mind. Disfigured children. Hundreds of them. Terra screamed at the terrible things she was seeing. Putting her hand over her mouth.

"What have you done?" She whispered.

Smiling in deep thought of his offspring. "This is the future. Soon they will breed new life into this world so we may all feel and look alike. And we can all be the same monsters! "He laughed; head thrown back to show his nasty sharp teeth.

"No! You can't do this! You don't know what you are saying!" Terra tried to reason with him.

"Oh, but I do." McShane smiled. "Be happy about being their mother. They are going to need a mother. Because all children should have a mother!" He screamed and his face started to change and turn into a gray wolf with black eyes.

Terra's fear was making him excited. He lunged for her, before she could move, he was on her. Pinned down on the bed, his eyes looking in hers and his drool running down the side of her face. McShane bit her shoulder just enough to mark her as she passed out again. Standing up pleased with himself." You belong to me now." He said as he left the room.

CHAPTER 9

"BLOOD OF THE INNOCENT"

March 17, 1877

"Happy spring equinox!" Mayola smiled in the early morning sun. "Wakeup, Terra or you will miss the sunrise." Mayola put the morning tea and biscuits on the table and began opening all the curtains in their cottage to let the new light in that was sure to bring about renewal, fertility, and rebirth of the new year.

Stumbling out of bed, Terra smiled at her mother's very presence. Mayola was a breath of sunshine all her own. Kind, sweet and gentle. But a force to be reckoned with.

"Good morning ma! Would you like to come into town with me today?" Terra asked walking into the living room. "I need a few things for the gathering tonight."

"Yes. I think I need a few things myself." Mayola smiled back at her only child. The air was sweet on this beautiful morning. And a sense of happiness filled them. Walkin the two miles into town was so worth it today. Picking flowers along the way for medicines and tinctures proved to be fruit full and would help them all when the weather cooled off again.

"Terra. We must discuss the future. We need to finish our plan soon." Mayola smiled. She knew there were spies all around. She could feel them. "We will talk more tomorrow after the celebration." Terra hugged her mother and smiled back at her. "For today we celebrate!" Both laughing and enjoying the morning they made their way to the marketplace.

"Look at these silks, Terra. I think this blue is a great color for tonight." Mayola said looking up. "Terra?" Walking to the other side of the store, Mayola looked out the window. Setting down the basket, she walked outside. "Terra! Where are you?"

"Well, hello Mayola." Froze in place, Mayola turned around to face the voice behind her. Two henchmen grabbed her and threw her in the carriage before she could even protest.

Terra woke up to a doctor standing over her. "What happened?"

"Well, well she is awake." The doctor announced. "How are you feeling Terra?"

"Why am I strapped down? And where is my mother?" Terra asked.

"Your mother is fine for the moment. You on the other hand need rest for a few days but the incision site will heal rather quickly." He smiled but it seemed almost mean.

"What does that mean? Where is she? What incision? Did I fall? What's happening?" Terra started pulling at the tie downs and shaking the bed.

"There, there now. We don't want to upset the surgery site." The nurse smiled then pushed a needle in Terra's arm.

April 1, 1877

Terra sat up looking around her bedroom. Blinking. Yawning. Unsure of why she felt so strange. "Mom. Mom!" Terra got up and ran to her mom's room. There was Mayola laying down.

"What happened?" Mayola stretched. "I feel so strange."

"I believe we were kidnapped by the mayor." Terra said quietly. Sitting on the bed, Terra hugged her mother tightly. "But I'm not sure what it means yet.

CHAPTER 10

"MY SIDE OF THE POND"

December 24, 1799

"Oh, love your burning up. The doctor is on his way." Hank could sense Scarlett's pain. No longer conscious, he knew she might not make it.

Knock. Knock. Opening the door, Hank shook the doctor's hand. "Where is she?"

A few minutes went by. The doctor came back to the kitchen. "She has the fever sir. Only a quarter of my patience is showing improvement. I'm sorry. Only time will tell. Keep a cold cloth on her face. Change it frequently. Stay home until you know for sure you don't have it."

After the doctor left, Hank sent a telegram for Boone.

October 11, 1802

"Boone! Hank!" Macki went back and forth to check on each man as she tried to figure out how to get help without them dying until she got back. "Help me!" Macki cried as she laid her head on Boone's chest. She could hear his heart slowing from blood loss.

Macki untied Hank. He seemed to be unconscious but not dead or dying. "Hank, wake up! Hank, please wake up." Macki spit in his eyeball to jump start his brain and fairy dust in his nose to make him sneeze. "Oh man, my first assignment and everyone dies! Macki cried, her beautiful little face crinkled in pain. As tears fell on Boone's chest, his wound started to glow. After a few moments his breathing evened out and he started making whimpering sounds. Then it stopped. Hours went by. Then a few days. "They need food. "Macki thought, then she took off. "Twelve frogs should do it." She smiled. Macki ate and sliced up the frogs then put them next to Hank and Boone's faces. Both famished and healing, they sat up and started eating. Macki smiled "Finally! Your awake!" Her little fangs showed fully as Boone's eyes shined bright and full of rage. Boone stood up as a wolf in his full glory and howled so loudly it shook the entire house. Full of anger, he howled until he was completely out of breath. Hank walked up slowly and howled in turn as if to except the mission.

October 12, 1803

"Dad." Boone started. "I know you have a lot of explaining to do. But, right now, I need you to help me save Terra and find this treasure.

"I promise we will fix this son. But there are some things we need to discuss. McShane is my half-brother. He is about 200 years old and as evil as they come.

He doesn't have many weaknesses. He is very vain though. And we might be able to use that to our advantage. Macki, we need to get to the fairy door." Hank smiled at Macki from one soldier to another.

"My pleasure!" Macki smiled proudly.

THE COWBOY AND THE WITCH

The next morning ready with supplies and a plan. Boone, Hank and Macki set out to save Terra.

The fairy door looked a little strange to Boone. Macki said a few words in Fae, and the door started to light up. It almost looked alive. It seemed to sway or move with a wind you couldn't feel. When Macki came back with the news it was open, she told them how to get through.

Boone looked down and laughed as Macki explained the price to open the fairy door.

"You want me to do what?" Boone cringed.

"I need you to donate some of your future kin in this jar. Boone narrowed his eyes. "Hey, I don't make the rules. Come on, we must hurry." Macki tapped her foot pushing the jar into Boone's hands.

"Do I look like a person that can hurry that." Boone mumbled and rolled his eyes as he walked away.

Walking through the door Hank had a smirk. "What's so funny pops?" Boone looked super annoyed.

"Oh nothing." Hank snickered.

Boone could feel his body morphing from one transformation to another as his body was hurled through the time warp forcing him to acknowledge all the impossibles that are very much possible.

"Mommy! Mommy wake up! We must go now."

Terra sat straight up, taking a deep breath. Looking around. Realizing she is alone, and then the sharp pain in her shoulder hurt." Ow. That jerk bit me!" She said through clenched teeth. Pulling on her pants, the map! It's still in my pocket! Blinking hard her eyes began focusing in the dark. "Oh no sir, you will not win. I will beat you. "Terra pulled all her strength together and zapped the door open with a light click. Armed with a small knife and new night vision she recently acquired from a nasty bite. Terra set off into the night, as quiet as a mouse. Once out of the house she ran towards the river. It was her only hope.

Get to that treasure. Passing the stable she looked inside for people. Nice and quiet. Stealing a horse might be fun. Terra opened the first stall to a beautiful black mare. The mare seemed to understand what she needed. Off into the night they went. Riding along the river they made it all the way to a hand-shaped bend in the river.

"Ok if I remember the map saying, West from the Harrow hand, you must float from here away from land."

"Boone!" Hank yelled.

"Ohhhhhh. I'm over here." Boone moaned as he rolled over to his stomach. "I think I'm going to be sick."

"Come on and quit playing on the ground. You're the big bad wolf." Hank laughed.

Boone caught her scent almost immediately. Something was off about it. "We go south from here." The smell of her sent Boone into a full run.

"Help me!" screamed Terra. Sitting on the top of a small shed. The 10-foot alligator lunged and hit the lean to shed with his massive head. "Ahhhhhhh!" Terra yelled as she threw her shoes at its head to no avail.

Boone came bursting through the bushes, in his full wolf, to tackle the gator. Clawing and biting until it stopped moving. Terra watched Boone and Hank change right before her eyes. Tears were running down her cheeks watching them. After she was sure the gator was dead, Terra climbed down and ran to Boone. Holding Boone's face and recognizing him in his beautiful wolf form on his first full moon.

"OH, Boone! You look as handsome as ever. "Terra cried as she hugged his huge neck. "I thought I would never see you again." Boone nudged her with a worried expression. "Yes, we must go."

October 13, 1877
3:18 am

On a pirogue going southwest of Harrow hand. We have an hour to find the Island of the Grande.

October 13, 1877
4:20 am

"Finally!" Terra sighs a breath of relief. "I see land."

Boone is ready to pounce in an instant on anyone or anything that's on this beach.

"We don't have much time till dawn." says Hank.

"And the eclipse starts at 10:15 am. So, let's not waste time. We need to look at the map and figure out how to find this place." Terra started to explain. "It's quite out here. "Terra looks around. "It's almost unnerving and it feels almost...."

"Ahhhhh!" Boone screams as he starts to turn from wolf back to his human form.

Birds flew off in the distance and the winds picked up as Macki appeared from thin air. With a cry of relief, Macki zips towards them. "Terra!" She yells in absolute joy. "You're alive! Boone! Oh, Boone! "Macki throws fairy dust at his head trying to ease the pain of the transition. But it's the way of the universe. The pain is how we connect and empathize with the world around us. Terra and Macki watch in amazement as Boone finishes changing from beast back to man. Hank stood guard over Boone's body while it struggled to come through his change.

CHAPTER 11

"THE CALVARY HAS ARRIVED"

5:00 am

The dawn is now breaking to reveal a determined crew from the magical world that has been bestowed upon them for the largest war in magical history.

"Hold up." Terra whispers in terror seeing the army march towards them.

"Finally!" Macki shakes with excitement. They have arrived.

"Who is they?" Terra asked

"Well, it's our army." Macki smiled proudly. "Once we got back to 1877, I knew we were going to need help."

"We sure do." Terra said, amazed at what she was seeing.

Fae in all shapes and sizes. Witches and goblins, flying beings. And Terra was sure she saw a mermaid. And to her absolute wonder, a pack of some of the largest wolves she had ever seen. Tears of relief started to fall. Now we have a real chance. Terra thought, closing her eyes and putting her hand on her belly. A warlock, named Kano stepped forward.

"Hello, miss Terra, we hear magnificent things about you." Kano smiled." We are here to help save the future of our universe. We are at your service." Kano bowed then says a few words in his beautiful Japanese language. And behind him was an entire Japanese army.

This is more than she could have hoped for. What a beautiful sight to behold. The army stopped right there in front of her on that beach ready to battle at a moment's notice.

"Let me start off by saying how grateful I am to see all of you." Terra said holding her heart. "We have no time to waste! We must find this treasure and put an end to this Mayor and his terror on our realms. He must be stopped at all costs, or our magic will be lost forever. He has done the unimaginable. He has murdered the innocent and poisoned our future with his perversions of life. We will not take any prisoners! "Terra screamed. Everyone cheered in unison." So, I ask you now, Will you let me lead you to a new way of life? One where we can coexist! One where our children can just be themselves! A life of Empathy and love. Shaking their heads and raising their arms and weapons in agreement. "Then let's go forward and end this thing for good." Terra said calmly as her eyes clouded then went back to brown.

Everyone shaking heads moved forward for their first assignments.

CHAPTER 12

"FINDERS KEEPERS"

October 13, 1877
(6am)

"**H**ugo! Where are you?" McShane screams. "Hugo! Come here! I swear I will cut your head off!" But Hugo was nowhere to be found.

"Terra is also gone, sir." Madam Dauphine lowered her head in fear.

"What! "McShane let out a wolf growl loud enough it shook the windows in the mansion.

"Her doorknob was broken from the inside when I went to check on her." Madam Dauphine said as she tried to back away from him.

The look on his face is a distorted hatred as he got within inches of her. "You will be punished for this." he hissed. After sniffing around her room and following her trail outside McShane burst through the front door. "Ralph!" He yells at his commander.

"Yes Sir!" Ralph salutes.

"Assemble the gargoyles and sirens. Meet me in the tower. Now!"

"Yes Sir. "He said as he ran off to signal them.

Hissing and moving around anxiously the gargoyles and sirens were ready to fly!

"Bring her back to me unharmed! Understand! Here is her shirt. Bring her back!" They all took turns getting her scent. Each one taking a good whiff until their pupils dilate. Then, taking turns flying out the window towards the river.

Shaking from the cold, Hugo finally pulls himself up on the beach of the isle of the Grand. "Must find the witch, must find the princess! Hugo chanted as he ran towards the scent of her.

Shouting and commotion brings Terra and Kano from the commander's tent.

"We found this little one coming towards the camp. "The large wolfman threw Hugo on the ground at Terra's feet. "He said he needs to talk to you. Do you know him? Want me to kill him? "The wolf grinned.

"Yes, I recognize him. "Terra said furiously. "Search the water, he is one of McShane's spies. Hugo stood up.

"What are you doing here?" Zano asked Hugo, raising his sword.

"I am Hugo. I knew your grandmother. I was your grandmother's servant all her life" Hugo said hanging his head. "I loved her more than my own life, until they took her from me." Tears now streamed down his scared-up face. "Mayor McShane took me as his prisoner when they took her from me. But when I realized who you were and what he was going to do.... Hugo's voice trailed off in pain. "My family swore an oath of servitude to your family hundreds of years ago. This has always been the way. Please believe me. I have information that will help you find the treasure and beat him, and he will come for you. For now, you bear his mark and carry his seed."

Everyone sucked in a breath at the new information. Terra froze at the acknowledgement. She knew they all deserved the truth of what they were up against.

"Yes Hugo. He bit me and yes, this is his seed I carry. Through witchcraft alone. The universe says this child will be the peacekeeper of this realm and the rest. This child must be protected. If McShane gets him, we are all doomed.

"Well Princess, I am here to help. I can find the treasure you seek." Hugo smiled sweetly.

"Princess?" Terra asked.

"Why yes." Hugo stated, as a matter of fact. "Your grandmother was the superior Witch queen of New Orleans. You are the last of her line, my princess. Why do you think the Gods chose you?" Hugo bowed his small body then kneeled before her as he promised his oath. "I will forever be yours." Then the ring on his finger started to glow. He looked up and smiled. "It's time to go now princess. The treasure you seek awaits. "Hugo stood and ran to the table to gobble up the bread and fish as fast as he could. Then smiled as he burped loudly. The smell was horrible. Hugo giggled as he rubbed his belly.

"Please explain, Hugo." Terra demanded.

"Your grandmother gave me this ring the day before they took her. It wasn't until now that I knew what it was for. This ring is your ring now. Just look at the stone." Hugo offered Terra the ring. It fit perfectly as she put it on her right middle finger. Immediately it started to glow. Staring in the crystal Terra could see an "X" and a pathway from the beach. A small wave of electricity went through her as her soul accepted the ring as her responsibility now. Her third eye opened as her human eyes stared to glow. Now she could actually see the path to the treasure.

"It's Underwater." Terra whispered. "Hugo." Terra turned to face him.

"Yes, my princess." He bowed.

Terra knelt to grab his small, battered hands. "Right now, for all to see, I want you to pledge your loyalty to my family again."

Hugo got on one knee.

"I, Hugo, of the northern waterways, last of my kind, promise to serve and protect you, Queen Terra Marie Poyadeaux, always and any kin that may follow from this day forth. Standing with his hand over his heart. "Hail to the Queen!" Hugo chanted.

"Hail to the Queen!" The army chanted together.

Terra felt a slight flutter in her belly as the little prince there also accepted Hugo's promise. Smiling Terra stood to her full 5 foot.

"Let's go forward and stop this evil for good!" She screamed.

Everyone cheered.

As they moved forward through the swamp they began to hear loud flutters in the distance. To Terra's horror the sky filled with large, winged creatures spitting fire and throwing stones.

The red siren spotted Terra and Hugo and sped towards them as they ran for cover.

Boone was running towards them and changed to his wolf in midair to catch the siren before it hurt the one, he loved. They hit the ground sliding into a tree. Boone could hear it gurgling as he ripped its throat out. Boone let out a terrifying howl, the other winged creatures flew around him.

The army showed up and started taking them out. A few of the larger gargoyles were able to grab some of our soldiers and carry them off into the morning sun.

It's about 10 am now and the eclipse is about to start. "Queen Terra?" Hugo whispers. "Look.

"Terra looks up towards the water. She can see a thin gold line appearing on the sand. She stands up to follow it. It seems to be making a connection to the line appearing in the water. "We need a boat. Now. "Terra commands.

Tails start swirling in the water. More and more swirls until there are hundreds. Slowly the Mer people start to emerge. They are so beautiful. All different colors shimmering in the morning light. The mermaid in blue was wearing a crown and motioned for her to come with them. Nodding, Terra and 12 of her soldiers get on the backs of the mermaids to the "X" she can now see in the water. Not sure what to expect, Terra and the soldiers are Surrounded by an air bubble as they start to descend to a sunken ship about 2 miles offshore. Finally! The treasure that will save us is within reach.

CHAPTER 13

"BEWARE OF THE SWAMP WITCH"

"What! Go back now! Get the horses and all the manpower we have. We ride in 15 minutes!" Mcshane screamed. "They have nowhere to go. And they did all the work." He laughed a crazy screaming laugh that will send shivers down your spine for generations.

Assembled and ready to march. McShane set off in the misty morning sun to get his revenge and rule all the realms.

Descending the stairs of the ship Terra could see a glow coming from underneath the captain's quarters.

"There. "She pointed. Pulling up ship boards Terra could see it. The trunk they had been looking for is here. It seemed almost unreal to have it. The markings looked familiar as Terra studied the trunk. Looking at the locking mechanism and size of the chest, Terra could only guess what could be inside of it.

"Attack! "McShane screams with delight as army against army collides on the sand. The fighting seemed to stretch across 2 miles of beach. The mermaids started to surface and grab the Henchman dragging them into the sea to their watery graves. Their screams could be heard for miles. Terra could see the men and the creatures being drug under the tides into the darkness as they emerged down the beach near the swamp. Sneaking on land to get Terra, and the trunk away from the beach before they are spotted.

Then the eclipse finished covering the sun and all was in darkness.

With the trunk across Boone's back, Hank and Terra ran into the swamp not really knowing which way to go except for Terra's sixth sense that they were headed towards the cottage of the swamp witch.

The silence that followed was deafening.

"I can feel her." McShane whispered to his commander. "She is headed North."

Frozen, Terra stopped to listen. She could sense McShane was looking for her. "Bite me." Terra grabbed Boone.

"Wait, what?" Boone frowned."

"He bit me, and he is tracking me. Maybe we can mask it if you bite me." Terra frowned.

"She's right." Hank shrugged.

"Can we hurry though." Macki chimed in. Hugo could only grunt at trying to keep up with her.

"Oh, my goodness! Yall made it!" Terra hugged them so hard.

"Come on they are about a mile behind us." Macki was clearly out of breath.

Boone handed the trunk to Hank. Then he grabbed Terra and put his hand over her mouth to muffle the scream he was sure to come. Boone bit down over the old bite wound just enough to taste her blood. Then he covered her cry with his lips. "I'm sorry." He said into her mouth.

Terra began whispering a chant to find the cottage and fainted from exhaustion. Boone picked up the tired and injured queen and headed further into the swamp.

"Spell to find my way"
Hermes, keeper of what disappears,
Here me now, open your divine ears.
What is lost, I now wish to find, help me to stop being blind.
Direct me to what I seek.
By earth, air, fire, and sea.

"Chant 9 times." Terra said as she lost consciousness.

Macki repeated the chant over and over until her mohawk pulled them to the west. Slowly and carefully, they creeped through the swamp in pitch black. Stopping to listen and smell the air often to make sure they were not being followed.

After an hour of walking.

"What is it you seek?" "The wind asked softly.

They stopped; hair raised on full alert now.

"Refuge please. We mean no harm." Macki pleaded.

Silence for a moment. Then the wind picked up and pushed them northwest to a clearing. "Come this way with the woman." Said the wind.

After 10 minutes the sun was starting to emerge through the clouds. Something was moving under the water now. Slowly coming towards them. Eyes started appearing watching, intrigued, investigating, waiting for one of them to slip into the brackish murky water. Then there it was. A cottage. Forged in wood and skin? It seemed to be alive. Or alert. Maybe it's just exhaustion.

"I don't know about this." Boone said as he froze at the scene in front of him.

"Come on." Hugo laughed. "This is the right place." Hugo knocked twice and waved his tiny arm in a circle very carefully and purposefully. The door opened.

The smell of lavender and mint filled the air. The smell was like a drug to Boone. He could feel the ecstasy coming. Oh, how wonderful. Boone smiled as he laid Terra on the bed and covered her up.

The small swamp witch appeared as the smell of lavender and mint dissipated.

"Hello everyone. I am Cordelia. Daughter of the sea." She smiled, looking at the sleeping Terra. "She looks just like her mother." You could see the look of love and longing in her weathered face. "Hugo, I see you are back to your loyalties." Cordelia smiled.

Hugo blushed, for Cordelia's mother was his greatest love.

"It's an honor to be back in your presence, Queen Cordelia." Hugo's blush deepened as he bowed his head to her.

Queen Cordelia bowed in remembrance of the past with her mother, and her sisters.

"Thank you, Hugo." Turning her attention to the tired faces in front of her.

"Anyone hungry?" She asked.

"Yes!" They all chimed in together. "Good. Let's eat while you fill me in on the plan." Boone, Hank and Macki breathe a sigh of relief to have another ally on their side.

The fighting ceased as the eclipse put them in total darkness. Everyone retreated to the camps they made in the bayou to regroup.

"Here's the maps you requested, sir." Kaven, McShane's first in command, said laying out the map across the makeshift table. The sun started creeping in the tent while they plotted out their next move.

"Feed the men, let them rest. We can do nothing more today except scout out the other side of the beach and the swamps for tracks. Look for any signs of them. They couldn't have gone very far in her condition. Go now!" McShane carefully studied the map for clues of where they could be.

CHAPTER 14

"THE AWAKENING"

"Zano, there are a few footprints off the western side of the beach. Small ones. Maybe the troll. I believe they survived, sir." Kale said.

"If she dies, we are all doomed." Zano lowered his head.

"We also found the enemies camp." Kale smiled with an eyebrow wiggle.

Zano knew exactly what that meant. "Attack at daylight?" Zano asked, already knowing the answer.

"Along with a few booby traps we set along the way." Kale shrugged. Short and stocky, Kale was as fierce and handsome as he was deadly. And smarter in war then most of the men Zano had the privilege of serving with.

With a firm plan in place, the troop of 7 set out in secret to wreak havoc on the enemy just for sport. Reaching the edge of the beach, Zano could see people and creatures hanging and disfigured along the tree line.

"That sick bastard." Kale said with disgust.

"He is an animal." Zano whispered with widening eyes at the monstrous view in front of him.

"No sir, even animals don't do this. This is pure evil. We must kill this man, or whatever he is." Kale was getting angrier by the minute. Kale caught movement at the east end of the beach coming towards them. Kale smiled. "Here we go."

Soft baby giggles and a slight flutter in her soul had Terra in a deep soothing sleep. She could see a little boy, then a teenager, then a man stood before her. "Hello mother. I am Remus Alwin, your son." He said in a deep smiling voice. "Now that you have the ring, and the chest, I can help us." Then a small baby splashing in bath water smiles up at Terra with beautiful clear blue eyes, black curly hair, and tan skin.

"Hello my son." Terra smiled. Warmth and happiness filled her. Terra new they were headed for the biggest fight of their lives. Terra also knew they had to win. The future depends on it.

Awake and looking around, Terra yawned and sat up. "Boone?" she whispered.

Boone looked over from the couch at her. When their eyes met, he knew he would protect her with his dying breath. "Hi there." He smiled.

"Hey." Terra smiled back.

"Good morning !" Cordelia smiled entering the room.

"Good morning." Terra and Boone said, still looking at each other.

"Terra. I am your great aunt, Cordelia. How are you feeling child."

"Nice to meet you. Thank you for taking us in." Terra Smiled.

The whole crew was now awake.

"I will have breakfast ready in a bit." Hugo hurried off to the kitchen with Macki close behind him.

After breakfast Boone asked. "So, what's next?"

Terra looked at each one of them. "I think our next move is to get this trunk open so we can see if there is anything in here, we can use."

Everyone walked over to the trunk that was sitting on the table. No one could read the old inscriptions written on the box. Nor have they ever seen a lock like the one that kept it closed.

"Mayor McShane!" Kaven yelled.

Kale came out of the swamp and grabbed Kaven around the waist, and they hit the ground, Zano grabbed Kaven's legs. Together they dragged him back into the swamp without making a sound. Kale tied him to a tree.

"Tell us what he's planning, or we will cut off your head, traitor!" Kale punched Kaven in the stomach a second time. Kaven laughing through bloody teeth.

"You can't beat him stupid! He's not of this world. He is fueled by evil from the underworld!"

"Oh, he can bleed and die. Everything can. Everything does. "Kale smiled. Kale loved a good fight. He was made for this.

"We need some of his blood. That's how we figure out his weakness." Zano decided.

"And just how do are we supposed to do that?" One soldier stood to argue.

"It's a suicide mission, sir! Maybe our entire army can, but one man?" Everyone argued as they tried to convince someone to take on this impossible task.

"Look someone has to get captured to get that close to him. Maybe bite him and spit it in a vile? Everything has a weakness." Zano tried to reason.

"I will go." Kale stood. "And I will use my brother as bait." He laughed.

"Kale, listen to me! He is only part man. And part something else. Some sort of monster. "Kaven shook his head.

"You know all about being a monster, don't you. "Kale said through gritted teeth

"Look Kale, we had a mother once..." Kale stopped and looked at him.

"Don't you dare speak of her." He warned. Your father killed our mother, and I will never forgive you for not stopping him.

"I'm sorry I couldn't save her, Kale. I will never be able to fix that. But I swear I never hurt her." Kaven tried to reason.

"If you're not a monster, then why do you fight in one's army?" Kale wanted to kill him right there and leave his body for them to find.

"I owed a debt to some very important people." He lowered his head in shame. "I know I do not deserve your forgiveness. But I will make this right, I promise."

Zano and Kale exchanged looks. "Fine." Kale said. "We will escort you."

"No!" Kaven argued." He will know. I can't explain it. I made you a promise. I will return."

CHAPTER 15

"COME OUT, COME OUT WHEREVER YOU ARE"

"Where have you been?" McShane asked calmly.

"I was on their trail sir. They definitely went into the swamp. We need to gather our troops to get on their trail before the rains set in." Kaven explained.

By 7am the McShane troops set off west to find the footprints that headed into the woods. "Let's go find my child." He smiled.

"We should attack now." Zano complained swatting mosquitos. There seemed to be millions of them. Kale was now rubbing mud on his skin to stop them from biting him.

"No, we pick them off one or two at a time, then...." A Loud scream rang out through the swamp. Zano stiffened as they listened to what sounded like a sure death scream. As they moved closer, the swamp seemed to be breathing and taking on a life of its own. There were ripples everywhere in the water. The trees were swaying ever so slightly. And it was unbearably quiet. Zano, Kale and the men they had with them decided to sit and wait. Another scream rang out through the swamp. Then rapid gun fire came from the north.

Kale pointed south. "They changed direction, let's get behind them."

"Did you hear that?" Hank stood up and went outside. "Sounds like gun fire." Boone looked out into the swamp. "It's time to go." Back inside Boone started putting provisions together.

"We must leave now. They are coming." Boone said.

"Go now." Said Queen Cordelia. "I will hold them off. I have a few scores to settle of my own." She smiled.

Gathering up all their things. Hank, Bonne, Macki, Terra, and Hugo set out North for New Orleans.

By 12:45 Terra was starving again. "Can we stop? "Terra asked. "I'm so hungry."

Boone lifted his head high to smell the air. Not feeling alarmed, he agreed. "30 minutes is all we can afford."

Macki and Hugo were also starving. They set off into the swamp, their love of swamp frogs was such a delicacy. Hugo shivered with delight as he jumped into the water to catch his first one. A large shadow came over the trees, Macki screamed. "Dive!"

Hugo dove deep into the water to escape. The siren went in fast and grabbed what she thought was that short traitor.

Coming up she was holding a small gator fighting and snapping at her face. She dropped it out of the sky to fall to its death as she readjusted to dive again.

"Bi mi fe, Ci te fit"
Bind my foe, cease their fight.

Macki's sweet voice rang out that only a dog could hear, but the siren crashed into the trees as Hugo was coming up for air. They both took off with 3 frogs and 1 small gator in tow.

"What is it?" Terra cried seeing the alarm on their faces.

"There was a siren, but I think Macki killed it, but I'm not sure. I'm not a doctor." Hugo was out of breath.

"Whoa, slow down." Terra hugged Macki and Hugo to try and calm them.

"They are searching for us. "Boone looked at Hank.

"I knew they would be. Come on dad, let's make sure it's dead."

10 minutes later...

Hank and Boone found the siren and tried to question it. Then tore it apart and threw her in the swamp for the wildlife.

"I can smell her faintly." McShane inhaled deeply. "She's been here recently." He looked around for signs of her or the ones she travels with, but to no avail. "Set this place on fire. I want them burned out." McShane pointed at Kaven.

"Yes sir." That was all he could say as he gave the orders on how to do it strategically.

CHAPTER 16

"Home Sweet Home"

October 15, 1877

"We must sneak into my mother's home. It's the one place we can rest and regroup without being found. "Terra walked as fast as she could.

The small cottage looked as it always did. Light blue with yellow trim, only it was dark and gloomy looking instead of the happiness that once thrived here. There was no smoke coming from the chimney. There were no pies cooling in the window and all the flowers in the yard and the windowsill have died.

"And it's far enough from the village to not alarm them." Hugo went inside.

Even though they were completely exhausted Terra and Macki decided to make the cottage safe with magic while the men found food for them.

Terra went into her mother's room to find her white robes and stripped off all of her clothes. Catching her swollen body in the mirror, she was surprised at how beautiful she looked in this condition. She put her hands on her naked stomach. "I will save us little one. We will win. I promise."

THE COWBOY AND THE WITCH

Making a salt ring around the cottage and using protection sigals, Terra felt that this would be enough until they can make a plan of attack.

"Algiz Rune" A Norse and Viking protection symbol. Keeps you safe from random unseen harm.

"The cross" Christian Celtic protection in all areas.

Naked except for the robes on, Terra walks around the cottage throwing black salt and drawing the sigals in the air with her right hand. The ring is glowing. She could hear her son and Macki chanting with her. Macki's sweet whimsical voice that sounds like music notes from a small child. The sigals turning gold as she completes each one.

"Goddess of protection hear my plea,
Keep this person away from me,
When they are near, they will feel pure pain,
The closer they are, the stronger the pain.
Keep this person away from me.
As I will, so mote it be.

"Oh, auntie Cordelia.' McShane said smiling. "I know she is here. I can feel you and sense you. "Closing his eyes and concentrating.

The cries of animals perishing all around them as the swamp went up in flames.

Cordelia stood before him. Nails out, hair flaring and water rushing in from the sea to cleanse the evil from her swamp. "Be gone you evil bastard!" She screamed in the night.

Catching him off guard. He stumbled into a tree, then shot a bolt of lightning at her singing her hair. A siren flew down grabbing Cordelia by her arms. Up they went into the blackening sky.

Now the cottage was visible in the flames. McShane burst into the cottage tearing it apart. "Terra!" He screamed into the night as it started to rain. Stomping out of the cottage he felt a sharp pain in his side as Cordelia Stabbed him as hard as she could burying the athame all the way to the handle. Battered and bruised she fell next to him and passed out.

Kaven was the first to get to them. He pulled out the athame and threw Aunt Cordelia over his shoulder and ran into the night. Running north along the shore the merpeople started emerging. "Give her to us, we will take care of her. We saw your Queen and her people head back north. Handing her over, the sea seemed to swallow them up. Not a ripple remained as they disappeared one by one.

Running north now Kevan started hearing unnatural bird sounds. "I Have it!" He yelled. Zano and Kale came running out of the woods to meet him.

"We saw what happened and follow you to the ocean." Kale admitted.

Zano smiled." Let's go find our queen."

"Wake up you fool." The spirit put its hand over McShane's side to try and heal him. This magic was strong. It might take days to get this to mend. McShane mumbled something about the mansion and his doctors new what to do.

CHAPTER 17

"THE COUNT DOWN"

"Mommy. Good morning mommy."

Terra stirred in her sleep. She could feel the heat coming from Boone's body. She could sense his comfort. So deep in sleep. Terra laid her head on his chest. "Just a few more minutes before the rest of the world wakes up. "She thought.

The smell of food made his stomach start waking up. He pulled Terra as close as he could and pushed his arousal on her leg. Terra giggled. Boone was fully awake now and very aware of her womanhood near him. Eyes still closed, he smiled and put his face right between her breasts. Terra relaxed into him as he explored her body in the early dawn light.

"I want you." he growled.

She slowly opened up to him. Boone kissed her face and breast and belly then decided to take a cold shower for fear of hurting her or the child. When he rolled over, Terra straddled him.

"Are you sure?" Boone asked. Rocking her hips back and forth, eyes darkening.

"Yes." was all she said as he pushed into her as slowly and quietly as he could.

Terra started moving in a dance as old as time. His release was so sweet. Terra smiled at the thought of this moment lasting forever. "Ame Soeur." (Soul mate).

He smiled back. "L'amour de ma vie." (The love of my life.)

After breakfast a soft knock on the door had everyone standing slowly and quietly grabbing weapons. Boone walked to the door with Hank next to him ready to pounce.

Hugo looked out the window then laughed out loud. "Ha! They survived." Pulling the door open, there stood Zano, Kale and Kaven, and the entire army ready for battle.

"Hi!" Kale smiled with his eyebrow wiggle.

"OMG, you found us!" Macki smiled excitedly. "I left enough clues. I thought I was going to have to go back and get you."

Zano hugged Terra. "Everyone ok?" he asked pointing at her belly.

"Yes! Not much longer, maybe a week or so." Terra smiled.

Boone shut the door and looked around. "What's the plan?"

"It's infected sir." The doctor announced.

"That's impossible." McShane said.

Pus was starting to ooze from the wound and fever and chills wracked his body.

"Well sir it's a magical wound. My medical degree can only do so much." The doctor said.

"Then sacrifice one of my offspring you idiots and make it go away, Or I will have you dismembered and send parts of you to your kin." He coughed and grunted at the pain in his side.

"Yes sir." The doctor slowly backed away from the bed and ran down the hallway to the staircase that would lead to the underground "House of Horror." It's what the workers that live in the mansion called it. The smell got stronger as you descended the stairs. Is this what hell looks like? Is this hell? It sure looks like what the books said it would be. The doctor shuddered at the thought of getting trapped down here. The dimly lit stairs lead to a big wooden door. Pulling the door open to reveal the smell of copper, feces, urine, bleach, alcohol, burnt skin and maybe an electric fire.

To the right is the lab where doctors worked endlessly to make these creatures, different poisons, and antidotes. Past that was another locked door where "They" Lived. There was a pool, toys, food, and bunkbeds set up camp style. It looked like a daycare setup for the deformed and mentally insane. They were anywhere from 5 foot to 7 foot tall. Pale because they had never been outside. It was hard to tell how old they were because of the deformities.

"He needs one to heal! Do it!" The doctor demanded before any of the other doctors could interject.

"One of the girls." They agreed. They heal the fastest. Just like a slaughterhouse, they grabbed the 5 foot one with eyes like his and one arm is smaller than the other, and no hair. "Number 276, female, age: 31." They recorded it out loud in the surgery room. The light drained out of her eyes as they drained the last drop of blood from her body. The doctors began taking out her left lung to replace the one on the mayor before he lost any more blood.

"Any luck opening the chest?" Zano asked.

"Not yet." Terra replied, "We are not sure how to open it."

"I don't know how much time we have but the mayor was injured badly when your aunt stuck this athame in his side." Kaven chuckled. Handing Zano the knife to inspect and try to figure out a solution to taking out McShane.

"We sent spies to his mansion to get some information on what's going on there." Zano smiled looking at the knife. Then looking at Kale.

"What we do know is A, he will attack again. B, He has probably figured out we are here by now. And C, we are ready to fight at a moment's notice my Queen." Kale said.

Heavily sighing Terra new there would be a lot of death to bring forth this new life. Walking up to the trunk her ring starts to glow. Somethings different.

"How do we open this chest my child? Tell me how to save us." A silent tear fell as she closed her eyes and touched her belly.

"The willing blood of the innocent will save us.
The sacrifice of the unimaginable will sink us."

The wind whispered softly. Terra opened her eyes. Everyone was staring at her. The chest was hovering 6 inches off the table like someone was holding it. Taking a deep breathe Terra raised her hands to the sky. Chanting Terra's eyes went white.

"I call to,Bertcha, Goddess of keys,
Unlock the chest before me,
By my blood I swear to thee,
To harm none before or behind me,
I hold the lock, and I am the key,
Please open this lock for me,
As I will so mote it be.

Keys started to rattle.

"Blessed be my queen." The wind whispered back.

The chest opened and a light so bright came out that it was blinding. With watery eyes in awe struck silence Terra peered inside.

No one dared breathe for fear of breaking the beautiful sight before them. Was she a goddess? A Ghost? An Ancestor?

"Hello Queen Terra." Bertcha said in her angelic voice. "We have been waiting for you." She said handing the chest to Terra.

Something happens to you when you stand before the divine. You are overcome with the profound feeling of love and happiness.

A gift of hope and peace. Time seems to completely stop to allow you to bask in its beauty.

Then another divine appears.

"Hello Queen Terra. I am King Solomon. We gift you these as a promise to protect the people. Protect the lands. Protect the realms. Along with all living creatures on land as well as the sea. The ones before you and the ones behind you. And you must promise to protect Remus, the protector of the worlds. The all divine." he said as he laid his hands on Terra's belly.

Although she couldn't feel his hands, there was a warm sensation that swept through her. Closing her eyes and accepting the divine gifts that had been bestowed upon her. She could feel Remus accept his future responsibilities. Calm and happy. A hush and sleepiness came over the army. Everyone laid down right where they stood. And slept the most restful sleep. Even Macki had fallen asleep curled up on Kale's back.

The chest was now on the table for Terra. While everyone dreamed, Terra planned.

A Chakra wand- Carved from a dragon's tooth.

Cloak- White / invisibility

Athame- Made from dragon fire hitting sand, and dragon fire hitting rock.

Ring bracelet- 5 rings that attach to a gold bracelet. Earthe, air, fire, water, the world

Grimoire- World book of spells. Made from witch hair and dragon skin. The clasp is a dragon tooth. The buckle is gold from the forbidden mountains.

When a witch dies, their book of shadows bonds to this book, unless gifted to another. Except 1 spell. At least 1 goes to the book as payment to the afterlife. In magic, nothing is free.

October 29, 1877

"Ah, mayor should you be up?" The doctor came in to check on him.

"I feel fantastic!" McShane laughed running towards the towers. Eyes glowing red and seething with hate. He gathers his generals.

"We just got word where they are hiding. Gather anyone old enough to fight. Gather food and get the doctor. We leave at dawn!" Mcshane clapped his hands together in anticipation.

Down below them the offspring are restless and ready to be let out as the veil starts to thin. They are ready to be let out into the waking world.

CHAPTER 18

"ALL ISN'T FAIR IN LOVE OR WAR"

The army of Queen Terra began to awaken.
Terra stands watch as they start to sit up and stretch. Everything is different now.

"Good morning to you all. Today is a day we have been waiting for. The day we prepare to take back our homes, our families, our lives. Tomorrow we must be ready to fight for our right to survive. Tomorrow we must fight this evil, so it does not continue to wreak havoc on our lands, or our children. You have been handpicked to be a part of history. Some of you will not return, but I promise you this. You will not be alone. We will fight as one! We will win! So today, eat, and hug your loved ones. For tomorrow, we fight!" Terra throws her fist in the air.

The army shouts with war cries. "All hail Queen Terra!"

Sitting around the table.

"Queen Terra." Zano begins. "We have a sample of McShane's blood. We are testing it for weaknesses.

Hugo snorts. "He's very vain. He believes he's indestructible. And he is driven by the underworld by the deals he has made. The only way to beat him is to take what drives his life force. There is a pool under his mansion that is the gate to the underworld. At least that's the talk of the workers there.

"Then we must invade them before they find us." Terra is more determined than ever to end this.

"The spies have returned." Kale comes running in. "They are planning an attack at dawn."

"Then we attack tonight." Zano chimes in." We leave before midnight. We must get there quickly and quietly. But not all at once. We move in teams, so we do not alarm the villagers.

"Yes, we can attack from all directions. 4 Teams. North. South. East. West." Kale begins the plan of attack.

Squad 1: Leave right before midnight. You will attack from the water.

Squad 2: You will leave 1 hour after. You will come from the south.

Squad 3: You will leave 1 hour after squad 2 and you will attack from the north.

Squad 4: You will leave 30 minutes after they do and go right towards the front gate.

Everyone should be in place by the time you get there. This is war. We take no prisoners." "The mission is to find the pool and drain the pool. Kill the offspring. Kill the mayor. Burn the mansion. Got it! Good! Let's get to work." Kale smiled. This is his favorite part!

Out of breath, Hugo runs to the table. "Hold on! We were just finished testing his blood and you are not going to believe this! He is part wolf. And I'm pretty sure he is a direct descendant of Boone and Hank." Eyes wide, everyone turns to look at them.

"Hold on now, he is the bastard son of my mad father." Hank tried explaining. But he could see the doubt in their eyes. "Don't get any ideas of us growing up together. I am older than him. We have different mothers.

"Until we can be sure, we must keep our queen safe." Zano explains.

"Hold them." Kale says with disbelief. "Why didn't you say something sooner? Why all the secrecy?"

"I need their blood so I can test it." Hugo Held up the tubes.

"We didn't think it would matter. "Boone said through clenched teeth.

"Everything matters." Kale said running his hands through his hair. Terra didn't say a word while the tears ran down her cheek..

10:45 pm

"Ok squad 1. Go quietly. You have your maps and each other. "Kale helps the men get started in the right direction to the mansion.

"Looks like they are definitely family." Hugo said sadly.

"But will they betray me?" Terra asked still in disbelief.

"I don't think so my queen." Hugo hugs her.

"Ok men let's go! You will move south to come up the back entrance. We take no prisoners. Kill everyone. "The gleam in Kale's eyes says he doesn't care if he dies as long as he gets to fight.

Alarms started roaring to life when the screams started reaching inland. "Mayor McShane! We are under attack!" General Breaux ran towards the first-floor half dressed.

A nasty smile runs across his face as he sits up and claps his hands together. "It's time." He starts to laugh as the screaming gets closer.

"Let us go Hugo! "Boone yells. He could feel his body trying to shift but the silver chains would not allow it. "I love her, and you know it! I promised an oath to her! It will kill me if I break it! Please!" He howled in pain.

"Troop 3 go through the north gate. I feel like we should move now! "Something wasn't right. I'm going with troop 3. Zano, you take troop 4." Kale's gut was never wrong.

"Yes sir, we will be right behind you." Zano promised.

When they neared the mansion, it was totally quiet. Something was wrong. They decided to retreat to the water. Then all hell broke loose. Big, disfigured creatures came out of the dark screaming and swinging axes and swords. The torches all lit up all around the grounds. They could see some of their army tied to poles, and some lay on the ground.

Terra watched her last squad march away then she ran to Boone and Hank's tent.

"We have to go now!" She said pulling off the silver chains. With the cloak of invisibility and her sword, off they went into the night.

The war cries could be heard for miles as they neared the mansion.

"We have breached the mansion my queen!" Hugo and Macki came running towards her. Stopping to stare at each other when they realized Boone and Hank were with Terra.

"We found a way in." Hugo and Macki lead them to an outside stair well that went to the basement. Kale saw them disappear into the mansion.

"They are inside! Now for step 2!" Zano winked in acknowledgement. With bloodstained faces and a newfound strength, they kept fighting.

At the bottom of the stairs, the smell hit them.

"Ughh. I think I'm going to be sick." Terra cried turning white.

Boone could see the pieces of human flesh laying all over the clinic.

"Come on, we have to find the pool." Hugo pulled Terra down the hallway.

The medical room was bad, but the next room looked like children lived here. It looks innocent with the bunkbeds and toys, but it was tainted with the smell of death. Toys and food and soiled clothes littered the floor. Terra feels sad in here and holds her stomach. The next room is cooler but darker and musty. Down the last set of stairs is a warm room with a pool in it made of rock.

"We found it my queen." Hugo announces quietly. It is bubbling and dark, almost gray water. It feels lonely and creepy in here. Movement in the corner catches Terra's attention.

"You did it Hugo!" McShane smiles.

"What?" Terra stares in disbelief.

"No, my queen I would never betray you." Hugo starts to shake backing up to her.

"No matter." McShane grins and lunges at her.

Hank charges him at the same time, changing in midair they start tearing at each other's fur. Boone changes and jumps in only to be thrown against the wall.

Terra jumps in the water to look for the plug.

"Nooooooo!" Hugo screams.

The clouds outside darken and the sky starts to rumble. The fighting stops for a moment and time seems to stand still. Jumping in the pool after her, Boone is willing to sacrifice himself to save her. The pool starts to swirl backwards sending electricity through the room.

Terra screams when the first pain shoots up her right side. In slow motion another scream rips from her when another pain shoots up her back. "The baby is coming!" She starts to pant. She regains her balance. "Find the plug! And hurry!"

"It's too late!" Mcshane laughs. "You lost!"

Hank grabs him by the throat, and they land in the pool with Terra and Boone. Boone rips McShane's arm off. Hank starts tearing him apart. Terra slides out the pool dripping in red water and yelling at Hugo to find a way to stop the pool. It swirls faster and faster until Hank and Boone disappear. The water starts to boil over and McShane's body parts start overflowing into the floor.

"We gotta go now!" Terra screams.

Hugo throws the wolf coin in the water to pay for McShane's way, so they keep him in the underworld this time. Hugo turns and starts running towards her and disappears. Lightning struck the mansion. Terra disappeared. All the monsters start running back to the mansion. Terra's army chases them until they realize the mansion is sinking.

"Run!" Zano screams. "Go Now!" The mansion is now blazing on fire as the ground swallows it up.

October 31, 1803

"Terra!" Boone cries running towards the river. "Wait! Please." Hitting his knees. Reaching for the love that is lost to him forever.

October 31, 1877

"AAAAHHHHHH." Terra screams. I can't do this anymore! I'm so tired!"

"It's ok Queen Terra, we are all here." Macki smiles to reassure her.

"Where are we?" Terra asked completely exhausted.

"We are nowhere my child." Mayola smiled, rubbing her daughter's hair.

"Oh mom! I miss you! "Terra smiled faintly.

"Hang on my child. Almost there."

"Push Terra! One more time!' Aunt Cordelia is ready to catch the baby.

"Now!" Completely spent, a tiny cry finally pierces the night.

Surrounded by her ancestors and the divine.

12:01 on November 1, 1877, Remus Paul Alwin was born of the Poyadeaux clan from south of the lake.

CHAPTER 19

"PURPLE IS FOR BRAVERY"

December 16, 1877

"Congratulations, Officer Macki." Terra shakes her hand as she walks on stage to receive her new badge of honor for her outstanding bravery in war.

"Thank you to all our soldiers. Without you, we would not be here today. I know in my heart we will heal. Our realms will move forward and work together for all our futures. I look forward to future treaties and alliances with the new leaders of our lands. We are all responsible for the health, wealth and wellbeing of our people. And we promise to keep out those who would harm us." Terra waved at the soldiers and leaders before her.

"Everyone please stand. Put up your left hand. Put your right hand over your heart and repeat after me."

> Bide the Wiccan Law ye must,
> In perfect love and perfect trust.
> Eight words the Wiccan Rede fulfil:
> An' ye harm none, do what ye will.
> What ye sends forth comes back to thee,
> So ever mind the Rule of Three.
> Follow this with mind and heart.
> Merry ye meet and merry ye part.

EPILOGUE

December 25, 1803

"We have company." Hank smiled.

"Tell them to go away." Boone growled working tirelessly to rebuild his barn.

A familiar scent caught his attention. Nose all the way up in the air Boone inhaled deep. Eyes almost glowing. Her! Hair raised up on his neck, he starts running as fast as he could towards her scent.

Hecate World Grimoire

"As above, so below"

Whatever happens in a higher realm or plane of existence is reflected in a lower realm.

You have been given a gift of the universe at your fingertips. Use it wisely. When you cease to exist on this plane, your responsibility to return that gift will be rewarded with your ability to rest within the lower plane.

"An ye harm none, do what ye will."

Charms

Charms are to protect and bring about good luck

Cleanse- charge-or consecrate before using

Witches charm- Protection from dark magic

Talisman- Inscribed ring or stone to help with magic powers

Amulet- Protection against evil, danger, disease.

Pick your charm or maybe it will pick you.

Color

Pick a color for magic. Candles, clothe, jewelry, or anything you need to represent for the spell.

White- Purity, Peace, Virginity

Black- Binding, Protection, Repels negativity

Red- Element of fire, Blood, Strength

Green- Element of earth, Healing, Growth, Money

Purple- Spiritual power, Hidden Knowledge, Psychic ability

Brown- Special favor, Relationships, House, animals

Orange- General success, Property deals, Legal matters, Justice

Yellow- The element of air, The sun, Memory, Intelligence

Gray/ silver- The Goddess, Astral energy, Telepathy, Dreams

Familiar

Every magical being has a familiar. They usually pick you. Be patient.

Cats- most common

Dogs- common

Birds- owls, ravens, hawks

Frogs or Toads- Common

Rats- common

Ferrets- common

Butterflies- Less common

Pig, Sheep, Horses- Less common

Anything can potentially be a familiar. Don't forget to name them.

Herbs

Sage- purification, cleansing, protection

Lavender- relaxation, peace, love

Rosemary- Memory, focus, healing

Mugwort- dreaming, divination, psychic abilities

Yarrow- healing, protection, divination

Vervain- luck, positive energy, harmony

Bay leaf- Success, ambition, achievement

Rose- Love, beauty, romance

Peppermint- energy, vitality, clarity

Cinnamon- Abundance, prosperity, warmth

Don't forget to blow Cinnamon through your front door on the first of every month for abundance lest ye be sorry!

Incense

Basil- Energy, physical strength

Sandalwood- Protection, Casting out negative energy

Vanilla- mental health, affection

Jasmine- purification, dreams, love

Cinnamon- sexual desire, healing, money

Lavender- affection, peacefulness, sleep

Dragon's blood- amplifies effects of rituals

Coconut- love, chastity, fertility

Frankincense- prosperity, growth, confidence, an offering to the Gods

Myrrh- Invoke divine feminine

Patchouli- passion and romance

Vampire blood- amplifies any ritual, passion, lust, lunar magic, seeing in the dark

Incense enhances your spiritual journey; they help you awaken the senses. Use them to increase your focus, and improve meditation. And don't forget to use sage before any ritual to aid in cleansing and purifying the energy in a room.

Moon Water

Moon Water- Usually made during a full moon
Fill a glass bottle or jar with a lid
Set your intentions as you fill the bottle
Set outside during the full moon
Great for manifesting your desires
Use it in your rituals, add to bath water, cleanse and anoint
Collect before sunrise

Dear universe,

I humbly ask that you charge this moon water with happiness when add it to my coffee, laughter when I cleanse my face, and love when I bathe at night. I am so grateful for this chance to be a better person and may it show on the outside as well as the inside. So mote it be.

Or set whatever intention that you may need.

Sun Water

Sun Water- Usually made at midday

I use it to charge my crystals

Purify, cleanse, invigorate or use as a life cycle in spells

Glass jar, set intentions, fill jar, set out at noon on a beautiful clear sunny day

This is a great way to empower spells and rituals, anoint things and bless things, it's great for spiritual empowerment

Get the jar from outside before it gets dark

Dear universe,

I humbly ask for your aid in cleansing this jar for future use in my rituals for a better outcome. I set these intentions with gratitude and a happy alignment with myself and others.

So mote it be.

Oils

Bergamot- money, success, strength, confidence, intuition

Chamomile- harmony, calm, uplifting, meditation, prosperity

Cinnamon- love, protection, abundance, prosperity

Sage- protection, health, longevity, purification, grounding, wisdom

Eucalyptus- healing, purification, growth

Lavender- happiness, relaxation

Lemon- Energy, cleansing, awareness

Patchouli- Fertility, growth, love, passion, success

Peppermint- protection, focus, purification, healing

Sweet Orange- Divination, clarity, Joy

Thyme- courage, ambition, clairvoyance, honoring ancestors

Use these in addition to any spells when you need an extra boost. Also, can be added to witch jars, sachets, anointing tools, casting circles, Ritual baths, Etc.

Witch Jars

Clear your mind and decide why you need this

Now find the size jar according to need

Collect the things you believe might aid in the spell work- hair, herbs, oils, intention, personal items, etc.

Set the intention for use

Example- if friend or foe decide to gossip, I may simply put a picture of them, some vinegar, maybe a jalapeno.

Dear universe,

Hear my plea, the friend or foe has gossiped and deceived me.

Please make it stop, and send it back to thee, times 3.

So mote it be

Some keep jars to reuse

I prefer a fresh one with each use

So collect those glass jars from everywhere you may go

Spiritual Bath

Cleanse your Aura / Energize you Spirit

Run some water on your favorite temp

Add the herbs, oils, moon / sun water, light the candles, say the intention out loud

Make sure your bathroom is clean before you start

Soak away sister

Listening to healing meditation music

I usually say- Today I wash away any negativity. I go to sleep and dream of a solution to anything I need an answer to. I am at peace with myself. I love myself. I am happy. I am free. I am excited about my future. I am strong enough. Thank you, universe, for another day to live.

Say positive affirmations only!

Witch Braid

By the knot of one, the spells begun

By the knot of two, it will come true

By the knot of three, so it shall be

By the strength of four, it is strengthened more

By the knot of five, so may it thrive

By the knot of six, this spell is fixed

By the knot of seven, be it powered by heaven

By the knot of eight, guide the hand of fate

By the knot of nine, the thing is mine

Set your intentions and think of the thing you want or need as your braiding

FYI- You can add colored ribbon, or hair to the braid for an extra kick

Magical House Keeping

Eww: Not everyone wants to do housekeeping, ever, of any kind, like never ever

Mostly because you are cleaning after other people and their disgusting habits

No! I don't to wipe up

No! Wash your own clothes since you don't like to bathe regularly

No! I will not wash your dishes with your spit everywhere

No! I refuse to take out the trash and wash the can it's in because you keep dropping food everywhere

Seriously! Where does it end.

Never! That's right. Keep the space clean and it helps keep the negativity out even though it causes some of it!

Be sure to make a spray bottle to add your favorite essential oils to! You can also add oils to the laundry, the mop water and the air vents, think happy thoughts as you clean

Happy House Keeping

Casting a Circle

Clean your space first of clutter and debris

Lighting a candle helps

Don't be lazy. Do everything with intention and purpose. And I do mean in your life to!

Intentions and purpose cause amazing things to happen! And now add consistency and you are now living your best life!

Anyway, I use ribbon to make a circle because I can choose intentions with the color of the ribbon and you will need a bell and a knife or athame

Next set out whatever herbs, oils, candles, personal items, please start using your imagination and believing in yourself and trust your instincts. I am sure if we can believe in ourselves for an hour wouldn't life be grand...

Anyway, make sure as you put all this amazing stuff together you are setting, your intentions. I know you are capable of doing two things at once. Trust yourself. If you can't trust yourself you need to read every book you can find on how to have a sense of humor. Cause you going to need it.

And now stand up tall and put your hands on your hips, smile, feel all that love and positivity radiating through your whole body when you stood up. That is pride. Yes, you just cast your first circle. Use your beautiful imagination. Every person's circle will look and feel different. It's ok. I promise. Once you cast the circle you need to "Draw down the moon."

Drawing down the Moon

Ring the bell 3 times

Hold knife or athame up in the air and close your eyes to visualize the knife/ athame piercing the moon and its electricity being drawn down to you into your third eye and charging your chakras.

This prepares you to see, feel, and experience the magic that you now possess

Once you are charged with the magic of the moon you can "call the quarters"

Calling the quarters

In the circle you cast are 4 corners East (Air) = incense

South (Fire) = Candle
West (Water) = Glass of water
North (Earth) = Salt

Move in a clockwise direction pointing athame

Drawing a star between the elements say aloud- I call to the spirits in the East

Hear me and be here with me now
I call to the spirits of the South
Hear me and be with me now
I call to the spirits of the West
Hear me and be with me now
I call to the spirits of the North
Hear me and be with me now

Hail to the four directions the circle is cast

Do what work needs to be done

Then close the circle

Closing the Circle

Dis miss any deities you may have called upon and thank them

Use athame to move clock wise through the star to undo the circle

Say "The circle is now open the ritual is complete"

So Mote it be

The 12 Zodiac Signs

Aris - March 20 - April 19

The Ram

The element of fire

Cardinal sign

Birthstone - Sapphire, Jasper, aquamarine, Topez, Diamond

Sign ruled by Mars

Soul mates - Leo, Sagittarius

Known for - Leaders, pioneers, passionate, energetic,

No No's - Impatient, Impulsive, Stubborn, attention seeking

Taurus - April 20 - May 20

The Bull

The element of earth

Birthstone - Emeralds

Sign is ruled by Venus

Soul mates - Virgo, Capricorn

Known for - They love material things, they are a great time, fun loving people, very grounded, love a home environment, very devoted to the people they love. Hard working. Sensual.

No No's - Extra stubborn, Jealous, Indulgent

Gemini - May 21 - June 21

The twin

The element of Air

Ruled by Mercury

Birthstone - Pearl, moonstone

Soul mate - Aquarius

Known for - Perceptive, often very funny, smart, passionate, extremely loyal, social

No No's - Their dual personality makes it hard for them to make a decision, impulsive, easily bored

Cancer - June 22 - July 22

The Crab

The element of water

Ruled by The Moon

Birthstone - Ruby

Soul mate - Virgo

Known for - Nurturing, intuition, comfort in routine

No No's - hyper emotional, temperamental, spiteful

Leo - July 23 - August 22

The lion

The element of fire

Ruled by the Sun

Birthstone- Peridot

Soul mate- Aquarius

Known for-Loyal, confident, creative, generous, brave

No No's- Self-centered, dramatic, stubborn

Virgo - August 23 - September 22

The maiden

Cardinal sign

The element of Earth

Ruled by Mercury

Birthstone- blue sapphire

Soul mate- Capricorn

Known for- Hard workers, analytical thinkers, logical, supportive

No No's- perfectionist, judgmental, Stubborn, over thinker

Libra - September 23 - October 22

The scales

The element of Air

Ruled by Venus

Birthstone - opal

Soul mate - Gemini, Aquarius

Known for-Strong moral compass, charm, beauty, well balanced personality, natural peacemakers

No No's-Indecisive because they want to please everyone

Scorpio - October 23 - November 21

The Scorpion

The element of Water

Ruled by Mars, Pluto

Birthstone - Topaz

Soul mate - Cancer, Pisces

Known for - loyalty, passion, deep commitment to loved ones, master of secrecy, very intuitive, good instincts

No No's - Anger, they do not lash out often but when they do it's deeply hurtful

Sagittarius - November 22 - December 21

The archer

The element of Fire

Ruled by Jupiter

Birthstone-Turquoise

Soulmate- Aries, Leo

Known for- Lively, passionate, smart, free spirited, adventures

No No's- overly blunt, commitment issues

Capricorn - December 22 - January 19

The Goat

The element of Earth

Ruled by Saturn

Birthstone- Garnet

Soulmate-Taurus, Virgo

Known for- Honest, hardworking, ambitious, Practical and determined

No No's- Insensitive, mean but funny, unforgiving, dark and moody

Aquarius - January 20 - February 18

The water bearer

The element of Air

Ruled by Uranus

Birthstone- Amethyst

Soulmate-Gemini

Known for- Independant, Creative with wonderful ideas

No No's- Stubborn, rebellious, emotionally distant

Pisces - February 19 - March 20

The Fish

The element of Water

Ruled by Neptune

Birthstone- Aquamarine

Soulmate- Cancer

Known for- creative, imaginative, nurturing

No No's- Playing the victim, daydreaming, focus on problems

To be continued.....

www.ingramcontent.com/pod-product-compliance
Lightning Source LLC
LaVergne TN
LVHW091531070526
838199LV00001B/19